THE CHRONICLES OF
NARNIA
THE LION, THE WITCH AND THE WARDROBE

Edmund's Struggle

HarperColli

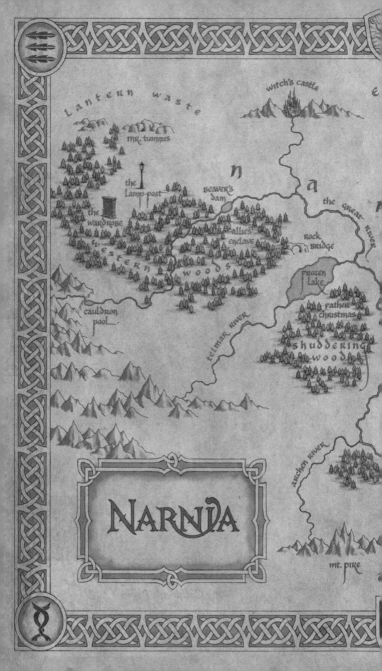

Edmund's Struggle: Under the Spell of the White Witch
text © 2005 C.S.Lewis Pte, Ltd

Photographs/art © 2005 Disney Enterprises, Inc.
and Walden Media, LLC

The Chronicles of Narnia®, Narnia® and all book titles, characters and locales
original to The Chronicles of Narnia are trademarks of C.S. Lewis Pte. Ltd.
Use without permission is strictly prohibited.

www.narnia.com

First published in Great Britain in 2005 by HarperCollins Children's Books.
HarperCollins Children's Books is a division
of HarperCollins Publishers Ltd.

1 3 5 7 9 10 8 6 4 2

0-00-773921-4

The HarperCollins website address is:
www.harpercollinschildrensbooks.co.uk

Printed and bound in Germany

Chapter One

High above London, the metal birds were dropping their bombs. Edmund Pevensie, young and unafraid, pressed his face close against the cold window in order to see the aeroplanes. Although there were many buildings on fire that night, the glass in the window felt like ice against Edmund's skin. Since the war began and his dad had left to fight, it had seemed like winter every day.

"Edmund, get away from there!" his mother cried. She hurried Edmund, his elder sister Susan and younger sister Lucy out of the back door towards the air raid shelter in the garden. Peter, the oldest of the four children, held the door open with one hand and tugged Edmund with the other. A thought passed through Edmund's mind. He broke free from his brother's grip. He had always been good at escaping. Whenever Peter and he used to play together, Edmund would manage to wriggle out of reach. Not that Peter and Edmund played any longer, since Peter had decided he was too old for children's games.

Edmund hurried into the house, with Peter running after him. On the mantelpiece stood a photograph of their father. Edmund reached towards it. At that moment the ground beneath his feet vanished and the whole room seemed to explode in a shower of glass. A bomb had exploded outside the window. Peter had tackled Edmund in the nick of time, saving him from injury … or worse.

"You little idiot!" shouted Peter as he grabbed Edmund's arm and pulled him back to the shelter. In Edmund's hand was the damaged photo of their dad.

The word 'idiot' rang in Edmund's ears days later as all four children sat on a train heading into the countryside. They were being sent from London for their safety and were to stay in a large house with Professor Kirke. Edmund felt that Peter was always being mean to him, calling him names and treating him like a little baby. One day, he thought to himself, I'll show Peter that I can be grown up too.

Edmund was still full of angry thoughts when the four Pevensie children stood nervously on the train platform waiting for the Professor to collect them. Instead of the Professor, an ogress of a housekeeper arrived called Mrs Macready. She wore a miserable expression. She showed the children around their new home and it seemed as though every sentence she spoke began with the word 'no'.

"No sliding on the banisters. No improper use of the dumb-waiter. No touching of the historical artefacts."

That first evening in the Professor's household, Edmund and his brother and sisters talked nervously about their new life. Lucy was very frightened about being away from home and far away from their mother. She was only eight years old. Although in his heart Edmund wanted to be positive and cheer his little sister up, he found himself only upsetting her more. Somehow, he always seemed to say the wrong thing. He knew what he said to Lucy might sound mean, but he was really only joking. It felt to him that Peter and Susan just wanted an excuse to order him around and to pretend they were Mum and Dad. Susan was only two years older than him anyway. It wasn't fair.

In his bed that night, Edmund thought how nice it would be if for once Peter and Susan had to do what he said, as opposed to the other way round.

"Gastrovascular," said Susan for the third time. Edmund gently banged his head against the table out of boredom. Outside the rain battered the window. Inside Susan was trying to make everyone play a dictionary quiz. Edmund thought he had never played such a dull game ever before in his life. Lucy suggested something different.

"We could always play hide and seek."

Edmund, before he could stop himself, made a nasty reply.

"Hide and seek's for children."

Again, he had managed to upset Lucy. He had not meant to. Edmund thought and realised that he could not think of one single nasty thing that Lucy had ever said to him. He hadn't always been so spiteful and unkind to his little sister. When he was younger he and Lucy had played together and the fact that he was older had not mattered. Now, he was embarrassed to play with her and thought, as an older brother, that it was his duty to tease her.

Peter insisted that they play hide and seek anyway. "Just like Peter to make me play a silly kid's game," thought Edmund crossly as he ran upstairs to hide. Edmund was especially annoyed that Peter got to seek first.

"One, two, three, four ..." said Peter.

Edmund found a hiding place behind a curtain.

He tried to make himself as small as possible and make his breathing slow and quiet. Suddenly, a hand pulled the curtain aside. It was Lucy, looking for a hiding place. "I was here first," Edmund hissed. Lucy disappeared.

"Ninety-nine, one hundred. Ready or not here I come!" shouted Peter. All of a sudden Lucy had reappeared and was shouting that she was back. Edmund tried to make her be quiet. At that exact moment, Peter found them.

"I'm not sure that you two have quite got the idea of this game," said Peter. Edmund felt dreadful. Not only had he been forced to play a kid's game and not only had he lost but he had also given Peter a chance to make a joke at his expense. And it was all Lucy's fault.

Lucy kept insisting that she had been gone for hours and had visited a magical land at the back of a wardrobe, called Narnia. She dragged Edmund, Susan and Peter to look at the wardrobe. Of course there was nothing there and Edmund saw his chance to get revenge on Lucy.

"I believe you," said Edmund. Lucy's face lit up. Then Edmund spitefully continued, "Didn't I tell you about the football field in the bathroom cupboard?"

Lucy ran away crying, but Edmund thought his joke had been very clever. Peter didn't and told Edmund off. This was the final straw for Edmund; he had had enough of Peter pretending to be better than him.

"You think you're Dad, but you're not." And then he ran from the room.

That night in bed Edmund lay staring at the ceiling. He was so angry with Peter and his sisters that he could not sleep. He wanted to make them sorry for treating him so badly. It seemed as though his heart was nothing more than a lump of ice.

His feelings towards his brother and sisters were cold and cruel; it was as if it were always winter inside of him. He thought of Lucy's stupid story about a world in the wardrobe. Only a real baby would imagine that sort of rubbish, thought Edmund.

Just then, he heard a noise. Someone was walking in the corridor outside. Edmund hurried to the door and peaked through a crack. It was Lucy! And she was walking towards the room with the wardrobe. Edmund had a thought nastier than any yet. He thought how funny it would be to follow her and tease her more about her crazy imaginary world.

Edmund began to creep after Lucy. He followed her down the corridor, staying out of sight. Finally, Lucy reached the room with the wardrobe and entered. Edmund waited a moment and then followed her in.

Inside the room there was nothing but the large wardrobe. The door was open slightly. Edmund thought she must be in there playing her silly games. He stepped in, preparing to scare her.

"Lucy… I hope you're not afraid of the daarrrk…"

However, it was Edmund who was about to get a fright. With each step the wardrobe seemed to get darker and colder and colder and darker until there was a … CRUNCH! Edmund's leg was wet. He looked down at his feet. Snow! He was standing in snow. In the middle of a wintry forest. He was in Lucy's baby world, except it wasn't a baby world at all. It was real. Everything Lucy had said was true. Edmund was in Narnia!

He did not have long to think about how embarrassing it would be to have to tell Peter and Susan that Lucy's nonsense world actually existed because all of a sudden, with a terrifying whooshing sound, a large white sleigh was racing towards him …

Chapter Two

With a whoosh and a fierce jangle of bells, Edmund's leg was caught by a large whip and he tumbled into a pile of snow. Before he knew what was happening he had been grabbed violently by an angry dwarf who was now holding a knife to his throat. When Edmund called for help, the dwarf tightened his grip.

"How dare you address the Queen of Narnia."

There didn't seem to be any escape for Edmund when he suddenly heard a female voice from the sleigh

"Stop!" The voice was hard and sharp like an icicle. A tall and beautiful woman stood up in the sleigh; it was the Queen of Narnia. "What is your name, Son of Adam?"

Trying his best not seem nearly as frightened as he really was, Edmund told the Queen his name and explained that he had been following his sister. The Queen's manner changed when Edmund mentioned his sister. She seemed scared of something. This made Edmund feel more talkative. He told the Queen that he was one of four children and that his sister Lucy had visited Narnia before. "She said she met some Faun, called Tumnus or something…"

The Queen became very friendly towards Edmund and invited him to sit in her sleigh. Edmund tried to be on his best behaviour; he had never met royalty before. The Queen offered him a warm drink and Edmund said, "Yes please," and then remembered to add, "your majesty."

The Queen took a small vial out from her robes. It looked like something from one of Edmund's chemistry lessons. The Queen poured one drop from the tube onto the snow. The snow began to melt. The steam rushed up and warmed Edmund's frozen face and there in the snow was a jewelled cup full of a lovely warm drink. Magic! Not only was the beautiful lady a Queen, she was also a magician or maybe, thought Edmund, a witch.

The dwarf, who was called Ginarrbrik, served

the drink to Edmund and called him "sir". Edmund felt very important. All Peter ever called him was "idiot". He bet no one had ever called Peter "sir".

The Queen told Edmund that her magic could provide him with anything he wished to eat. Now, Edmund had always had a special sweet tooth for one particular thing: Turkish Delight. And that is exactly what he asked for. The Queen produced a glittering box of Turkish Delight. Edmund tried a piece and the taste was like a hundred wonderful explosions in his mouth. Although he had eaten Turkish Delight many times before back home, he had never tried any that was quite like this. The only problem was that it tasted so good that the moment Edmund had finished one piece he had

to have another. And another. Very soon he had eaten all the Turkish Delight. Yet something still rumbled inside his stomach. He felt he needed more and found it very difficult to listen to what the Queen was saying.

"You know, Edmund, I have no children of my own. You're the sort of boy I could see one day becoming a Prince of Narnia. Or perhaps even a king."

This was the chance to show Peter and his sisters that he really was a grown-up.

"If I was king and they were my servants," thought Edmund, "they would have to do as I ordered." All Edmund had to do was bring his brother and sisters to the Queen's house. She pointed to where it was. Edmund's eyes followed the Queen's long white finger as it pointed to two ghostly hills in the distance. It didn't look like the kind of place Edmund wanted to visit.

"You'd like it there, Edmund," said the Queen, "it has rooms simply filled with Turkish Delight."

Something rumbled again deep inside of Edmund. He promised he would bring his brother and sisters to see her. Then, as suddenly as she had arrived, the Queen sped away in her white sleigh, leaving Edmund alone on the snow with a sick feeling in his stomach.

Edmund heard footsteps and turned to see Lucy. She was very pleased that Edmund had found Narnia as well, as this meant that Peter and Susan had to believe her story. Edmund didn't really want to listen to Lucy as she talked about Mr Tumnus. He felt unwell. Lucy took him by the hand and pulled him along until they were back in the Professor's house.

Lucy woke up Peter and Susan, telling them that her story of Narnia was true and that Edmund had been there too. Edmund felt a bit dizzy and dazed. He was aware that Lucy, Peter and Susan were all looking at him, waiting for him to say whether Narnia was real or not …

At this moment, the nasty feelings that had been growing inside Edmund ever since Dad had gone to fight in the war came to the surface and he heard his voice saying weakly, "I was just playing along. But you know how little children are. They just don't know when to stop pretending."

Lucy cried and ran from the room. Peter and Susan followed. All of them were upset and angry and Edmund felt … pleased.

"Wake up, Dolly Daydream," said Peter. Edmund realised that he had been standing with the cricket bat in his hand staring up at the Professor's house. He hadn't wanted to play outside. He had wanted to return to Narnia and eat some more of the Queen's Turkish Delight. He needed more Turkish Delight.

Peter bowled; Edmund swung the bat with all his power and … CRASH! SMASH! CLANG!

All four Pevensies stared at the broken window.

Inside, the children saw the damage the ball had done. It had smashed a window and knocked over a suit of armour. They heard Mrs Macready's footsteps and ran. They ran and ran and ran through the house, up all the stairs until there was only one room left to run to … the room with the wardrobe.

Edmund was pleased and he was even more pleased when Peter suggested they all hide in the wardrobe. Edmund thought that he would be able to keep his promise to the Queen … and get some more of that wonderful Turkish Delight.

The Pevensies climbed into the wardrobe and, sure enough, after a few steps, the wooden floor had turned to snow beneath their feet and all four children were in Narnia.

Peter decided that they should all follow Lucy to Mr Tumnus, the Faun's house. Edmund didn't want to meet Mr Tumnus. He had a strange feeling that by telling the Queen about Mr Tumnus' friendship with Lucy he had done something wrong. Edmund told himself not to be so foolish, but as they reached the Faun's house the sound of Lucy's happy voice stopped dead …

The door had been torn off.

Chapter Three

S omething was terribly wrong.
Mr Tumnus' door had been smashed to
pieces. Edmund followed his brother and
sisters into the house.

This can't be my fault, he thought. It has nothing
to do with me; I have never even met Mr Tumnus.

But he had told the Queen about Lucy's visit to
Mr Tumnus' house. Edmund began to get a sinking
feeling in his heart; that feeling was guilt.

The house looked as though a giant had picked it
up and shaken it. Everything was broken and
ruined. Plates and chairs and pictures and tables …
all lay on the floor in pieces.

Edmund saw a picture of an old faun. Something
in his soul told him that it was a picture of Mr
Tumnus' father and that it had been a very special
picture for Mr Tumnus. Now it was torn and
damaged, like everything else in the little house.
Edmund knew what it felt like to lose something
precious. The picture reminded him of something …
but he couldn't quite think what it was.

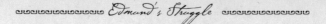

The feeling of guilt inside Edmund grew stronger.

Peter found a piece of paper and began to read it out,

"The Faun Tumnus is hereby charged with High Treason against her Imperial Majesty Jadis, Queen of Narnia for comforting her enemies and fraternising with Humans. Signed, Maugrim, Captain of the Secret Police."

It was the Queen who had ordered the destruction of Tumnus' house! Edmund looked around at the damage. This is all my fault, he thought.

"I'm the human. She must have found out he helped me," a sad voice said. However, it was not Edmund's voice but Lucy's. Edmund wanted to explain to Lucy that it wasn't her fault at all, but something held him back.

Peter tried to stop Lucy from crying. "Don't worry, Lu. We'll think of something."

The guilt inside Edmund was burning like a bonfire. He could feel it rising up through his body, up his throat and towards his mouth … He would tell the others his secret! But then, another feeling started. It began in his stomach, like hunger but deeper and stronger. He realised, if he told the others about his meeting with this Queen, with this White Witch, then he would never get to be a king of Narnia and would never get any more of that lovely, magical Turkish Delight. Yes, that was what mattered. Turkish Delight. He must get his brother and sisters to come with him to see the White Witch.

Edmund didn't want Peter and Susan to believe Lucy. He didn't want to believe Lucy. He wanted to

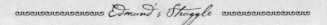

believe that Mr Tumnus was a bad person and that the White Witch had told him the truth. All his guilt vanished.

"Why," asked Edmund, "I mean, he's a criminal." Peter and Susan looked sharply at Edmund as he said this. "And how do we even know that the Queen's not in the right?"

The children left the house, uncertain what they should do, then they heard a very strange sound.

"Psst."

The sound itself was not so strange; it was a sound that anyone might make when trying to grab the attention of another person. What was strange was that the sound was being made by a very large beaver hiding in the forest trees.

The Beaver spoke with Lucy and Peter, but Edmund did not listen to them as they spoke. He could only listen to the rumbling in his stomach that repeated two words over and over again, "Turkish Delight. Turkish Delight."

As though in a dream, Edmund walked with his brother and sisters as they followed the Beaver over a frozen lake to his home in a large dam. All he knew was that they were walking further and further from the White Witch's house, from the dark hills and

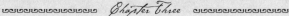

from the Turkish Delight. With every step, Edmund felt sicker and hungrier.

At the door to the Beaver's house, Edmund turned back for one more wishful glance at the black hills in the distance …

"Enjoying the scenery, are we?" asked the Beaver suspiciously.

Edmund smiled a sickly smile.

"Isn't there anything we can do to help Tumnus?" asked Peter, who was inside taking off his coat.

"They'll have taken him to the Witch's house," explained the Beaver. "And there's few who go through those gates ever come out again."

"But there is hope, dear," said Mrs Beaver, who was busily serving dinner.

"Oh, there's a right bit more than hope," said Mr Beaver. "Aslan..."

"Aslan is on the move," said the Beaver proudly. Behind him, his wife smiled and nodded.

Upon hearing the name Aslan, it seemed Edmund's knees turned to jelly and his head turned to rock, and deep inside him, grew a feeling of mysterious horror.

"He's only the King of the whole wood. The real King of Narnia!" the Beaver continued excitedly.

Edmund felt as though he was on a rocky boat and that a gigantic wave of cold water had washed over him. The White Witch had said that he would be king of Narnia … he, not Aslan!

The Beaver told the children that Aslan was waiting for them at the Stone Table. This meant nothing to Edmund or to his brother and sisters. The Beaver and his wife were shocked; they could not believe that the children had not heard of the Prophecy and so they recounted it.

"When Adam's flesh and Adam's bone,
Sits at Cair Paravel in throne,
The evil time will be over and done."

The Beaver explained the rhyme, saying that it meant when two boys and two girls arrive, Aslan would fight and beat the White Witch.

This seemed all wrong to Edmund. His stomach was screaming for more Turkish Delight. It was so loud, he felt sure that the others could hear it. It seemed as if an invisible chain was pulling him backwards, away from the Beaver's home and back to the White Witch's palace.

Quietly, Edmund moved to the door. He saw the door handle in his hand. With one gentle push

… he was outside in the snow.

The forest trees brushed against Edmund's skin, slapping his face. They seemed to push him forwards, away from his family. He was not sure whether he was running or being dragged. All he knew for sure was that he had to reach the White Witch and he had to have more Turkish Delight. He thought he could hear Peter's voice in the distance, calling his name.

He reached the foot of the hills and began to climb. At the top of the hill stood the White Witch's castle with its spires reaching up like the thorny branches of the trees. The rocky hill felt hard and cold under his fingers as he climbed. He heard his brother's voice on the wind again, but the wind suddenly seemed to blow away Peter's cries and instead whispered in Edmund's ear that he should hurry to the White Witch.

Finally, Edmund reached the castle. The terrible feeling in his stomach immediately seemed to get better as he stepped into the courtyard. The whole place was empty and reminded Edmund of the churchyard by his old school. Everything was still. There was not a

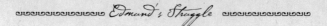

single sound. Yet Edmund felt as though he was being watched. He took a few steps, turned a corner and came face to face with … a lion.

Chapter Four

Being eaten by a lion did not feel like Edmund had expected. He thought that he would feel the warm breath of the animal and the sharp claws tearing at him, but he didn't feel anything at all. In fact, thought Edmund, being eaten by a lion feels exactly the same as standing in a cold castle with your eyes shut tight.

Edmund opened his eyes. He was still standing in the cold castle. The Lion was in front of him, exactly as it had been. He was not being eaten. Edmund thought that this was very strange, but stranger still was the fact that the Lion was not moving … indeed, the Lion did not even seem to be breathing!

Instead of a beautiful, bright yellow, the Lion's fur was a sad grey colour. Edmund reached out a hand to touch the still beast. Stone! The Lion was only a statue. Edmund picked up a piece of burnt wood and drew glasses and a moustache on the lion.

There were statues everywhere of every different type of animal Edmund had ever seen or heard of … and quite a few that he hadn't. Edmund walked up a flight of steps. At the top sat a large statue of a mean-looking wolf. Not afraid, Edmund lifted his leg to step over it when …

The wolf snarled to life. It was a real, grey wolf. It pinned Edmund to the wall and growled.

"Be still, stranger, or you'll never move again."

Terrified and unable to talk without stuttering, Edmund explained who he was. The wolf let go of Edmund and led him into a gigantic hall made

entirely of ice. Although the hall was beautiful and impressive, it seemed to Edmund to be very cold and scary. He was led past a long line of wolves; a single one of them could have eaten him up with one snap of their massive jaws.

At the end of the hall was a throne, also made of ice. Nervously, Edmund sat down. Although the throne was made of ice, Edmund did not feel cold. He felt happy. King Edmund, he thought proudly.

"Like it?" an icy voice enquired. It was the White Witch. At first she seemed pleased to see Edmund, then, she suddenly shouted at him, "how dare you come alone?" Edmund stuttered with fear. She was cross because Edmund had not brought his brother and sisters. He didn't want the Witch to be angry with him. He wanted to be King of Narnia. He wanted to eat more of the wonderful Turkish Delight.

"They're in the little house on the dam. With the Beavers."

As soon as Edmund had spoken these words, he felt worried. Was it right to tell the White Witch this? He could not forget the destruction of Mr Tumnus' house. Would the same happen to the Beavers now? Edmund pushed these thoughts out of his head … more important than anything was to stop the hunger in his belly.

"I was wondering, could I maybe have some Turkish Delight now?"

The White Witch looked at him and the room seemed to get even colder. Ginarrbrik appeared, wearing a grin that, to Edmund, looked quite wicked. The White Witch turned to the wolf and gave her orders.

"Maugrim. You know what to do." So this was Maugrim, the captain of the White Witch's secret police! Maugrim began to howl. The sound chilled Edmund to the bone. The other wolves began to howl and, as the noise grew, they all rushed out into the wintry night.

Edmund felt frozen. He had betrayed his brother and sisters and set the secret police on them.

The White Witch's dungeon stank of damp and disease. Edmund wished he had never met the Witch and never made his stupid deal with her. A voice shocked him out of his misery.

"You're Lucy Pevensie's brother," said the polite and gentle voice. It was Mr Tumnus. He was imprisoned in the next cell. Mr Tumnus spoke kindly to Edmund and asked how Lucy was. He clearly cared very much for her. Edmund couldn't look Mr Tumnus in the eye; he knew it was his fault that the good Faun had been captured. He only hoped that his brother and sisters had escaped the secret police.

The White Witch burst into the dungeon.

"Your little family was nowhere to be found," she yelled at Edmund. Although he was very frightened, he felt relieved that Peter, Susan and Lucy were safe … for the moment.

On the other hand, Edmund himself was not safe … now the White Witch had no use for him and she lifted up her magic wand. Edmund was terrified. He was sure that this was the end, unless … Suddenly, an idea came into his head.

"The Beaver said something about … Aslan?" Edmund blurted out in a panic. He immediately felt even guiltier than he had before. He had betrayed yet another person. At least, thought Edmund, if I don't tell her that Aslan is meeting my brother and sisters at the Stone Table, then I won't really have betrayed them. The White Witch tried to bully Edmund into giving her more information, but Mr Tumnus stood up for him. This angered the Witch and Edmund watched as Ginarrbrik dragged the Faun out of his cell. The White Witch, to torture Edmund and Mr Tumnus, told the Faun of Edmund's treachery.

"You're here because he turned you in. For sweets," she said with glee. Then, the Faun was gone.

Edmund was alone with only his guilt and his tears to keep him company.

Early next morning Ginarrbrik came to take Edmund from the cell. The White Witch wanted to hunt down Peter, Susan and Lucy and was going to use Edmund to help her. Edmund had spent the night building up his courage but Ginarrbrik hauled him through the house, towards the White Witch's sleigh, he saw Mr Tumnus. He had been turned into a stone statue. This good, kind Faun is dead, thought Edmund, and it's my fault. Before Edmund had a chance to think, Ginarrbrik dragged him outside. Edmund felt so sad inside, he thought that he did not deserve to escape.

Edmund wished he could have saved Mr Tumnus and made up for the bad things he had done. This was the only thought he had as he lay curled up in a ball on the floor of the White Witch's sleigh. He was so miserable that he did not notice that all over Narnia the ice was melting. Winter was ending.

The White Witch was rushing to catch Peter, Susan and Lucy who she believed to be meeting some allies, woodland creatures with a goat-like appearance called satyrs and a crafty fox deep in the forest. When the Witch arrived, she tried to force the Fox and Satyrs to betray the Pevensies, but they were too brave and true of heart.

Edmund watched their bravery and thought to himself that this was the correct way for a person to behave. He wanted to save the lives of these good creatures. Just as the White Witch was about to strike, he jumped out of the sleigh and shouted,

"Wait! Don't! The Stone Table. The Beaver said something about a Stone Table. That he has an army there."

Edmund thought he had done his first good deed for a long time, but he had not guessed at how cruel and evil the Witch could be. Even though he had told her what she needed to know, she still turned the Fox and Satyrs into stone. Edmund had failed again. He collapsed at the Witch's feet. She slapped his face and said, "Think about whose side you're on, Edmund. Mine..." She grabbed his face and turned it towards the statues. "...Or theirs."

Chapter Five

Edmund tried to rest his head on his chest but he could not. The ropes tied tight around him kept getting in the way. Neither could he put his head back and rest it against the tree to which he was tied. It was hopeless. Everything was hopeless. He had been travelling with the White Witch on foot as her sleigh could not be used now that all the ice had melted. He was exhausted.

"Is our Prince uncomfortable?" sneered Ginarrbrik. The dwarf hated Edmund and enjoyed teasing him. Edmund realised that this teasing reminded him of something … it reminded him of the way the he had teased Lucy. He promised that, should he make it back to his family, he would never ever tease his little sister again.

At that moment there was a terrible growling sound. A wolf arrived at the White Witch's camp in a panic. He rushed up to the White Witch's tent. Edmund felt pleased because bad news for the Witch must be good news for his brother and sisters.

Ginarrbrik took a step towards Edmund and drew his dagger. Edmund screwed his eyes shut, waiting for the sound of the dagger cutting through the air. Instead, he heard another sound. It was the sound of someone being hit over the head. Then there was the sound of ropes being cut and suddenly … he was free.

Edmund opened his eyes to see the strangest sight he had seen in his life. He was surrounded by creatures that were half man and half horse. Edmund had read about such creatures in fantasy books. They were Centaurs. Two Centaurs had knocked Ginarrbrik out and were tying him to the tree in Edmund's place.

Edmund could barely stay on his feet as he and the Centaurs hurried through the forest away from the Witch. The Centaurs gave him no sympathy. Edmund realised that everyone must think that he was a dreadful person for betraying his family, Aslan and the whole of Narnia. He imagined that Aslan would have him killed for his crimes, or at the very least, greatly punished.

They ran through the forest all night. To Edmund, the night seemed to last a year; he was so tired and ill. Now he was on his way to finally meet Aslan, whom everyone had talked about. Edmund was nervous. Surely this king would be fearsome and very angry with Edmund indeed.

Nothing could have prepared Edmund for Aslan. He had imagined an old man with a long grey beard or perhaps a tall warrior with a mighty sword and suit of armour. But Aslan was none of these things. He was more impressive and kingly. Aslan was a majestic lion, the largest creature that Edmund had ever seen. His fur was clean and bright and looked like the surface of the sun. As this impressive beast walked, he seemed to leave a trail of beautiful flames behind him. And his voice … his voice was so strong that it was almost as though he were talking directly into your heart.

Rather than being angry with Edmund and wanting to punish him, Aslan was pleased that Edmund had made it to the Stone Table alive and well. He took Edmund for a walk and they spoke for a long time about many things. Aslan seemed to know all of Edmund's secret thoughts, his hopes and his fears. It was as though Edmund's heart and mind were an open book to Aslan that he could read as easily as anyone else might read a storybook. Exactly what was said between them, nobody knows.

Edmund was very pleased to see his family again. He had missed them more than he thought possible. Lucy and Susan were pleased to see him too and each gave him a huge hug. Peter remained cold to Edmund. All Edmund wanted was a sign from his older brother that he was forgiven and that everything would be all right.

"Get some sleep," said Peter, "and Edmund ..."

Edmund's heart jumped up as he hoped to hear a kind word from his brother.

"... Try not wander off."

The next morning, there was breakfast! Edmund didn't think he would ever be so happy to see a plate of toast. He stuffed his face with bread and eggs. It was as if he had not eaten for a hundred years.

Susan, Lucy and Peter were arguing. Peter wanted the others to return home, now Edmund was safe, while he remained in Narnia to help Aslan.

Edmund listened to everything that was said. His head told him that it was sensible to go home, that they were small children not soldiers and that they shouldn't get involved in a battle where they could be injured, captured or even killed yet Edmund felt that he had been listening to his head for too long and that now it was time to listen to his heart.

"I've seen what the Witch can do. I helped her do it. I'm not leaving these people behind to suffer for it," he said with more seriousness than ever before in his life.

As he finished speaking his eyes met Peter's and he saw an unfamiliar look. Respect! He saw Peter respected him. It was becoming summer in Narnia, and Edmund's heart was warming also. He would stay and put right what he had done wrong.

The large metal sword was so much heavier in Edmund's hand than the sticks and broom handles he and Peter had used to play sword fights with back home.

That's right, thought Edmund, we aren't playing now. We are fighting for real. He and Peter were training; learning how to ride, how to defend and how to attack. Edmund knew that he was improving, but would he be ready when the time came?

Edmund heard a terrible horn sounding and felt fearful. He knew that sound. It was the White Witch. The Beaver explained, "The Witch has demanded a meeting with Aslan."

Edmund shivered as he watched her coming towards them, in a seat carried by four giants with only one eye each. Cyclops, thought Edmund.

"You have a traitor amongst you, Aslan. Have you forgotten the laws upon which Narnia is built? His blood is my property," declared the White Witch.

All Edmund's strength disappeared again. It was true. He was a traitor. Why should anybody risk their life for him?

"Try and take him then," a strong young voice replied. It was Peter! Edmund's strength returned as quickly as it had gone. He knew his brother loved him.

However, Aslan told the children that what the Witch said was true and then asked to speak with her alone.

All four children were anxious to know what would be decided, but none more so than Edmund. He knew what fate the White Witch would prepare for him. Death.

Chapter Six

To Edmund, Aslan and the White Witch's conversation seemed to last many, many days. In truth, it was only a few hours. When the pair returned, the Witch was smiling. This looked to Edmund to be a very bad sign, so he was surprised when Aslan announced, "she has renounced her claim on your brother's blood."

The children were all happy, but confused. Edmund didn't want to question what had taken place; he was just pleased that he was free of the Witch's power for ever.

But later that night, Edmund and Peter awoke with a start when a rush of green leaves swirled into their tent. Edmund rubbed the sleep from his eyes as the leaves formed themselves into the shape of a woman.

"Be still, my Princes," said the Dryad. "I bring grave news from your sisters..."

She then told them how Aslan had secretly gone to the Witch's camp and sacrificed himself as part of the agreement to free Edmund. As quickly as she had appeared, the Dryad left, leaving the two brothers in silence.

Edmund followed his brother to Aslan's tent. It was true. Their King and leader was gone. Peter was unable to bear the loss. He felt that he couldn't go into battle without Aslan. Edmund began to feel despair taking hold of him, as it had so many times since he had come to Narnia. But this time Edmund did not want to be beaten. This time he would choose hope over despair. It suddenly seemed clear to Edmund what needed to be done; he needed to give Peter hope so that Peter could lead their army to victory. In his heart, Edmund could hear an echo of Aslan's mighty roar and it warmed him to the tips of his toes.

Edmund summoned up all the positive feelings in his heart and soul and said, "There's an army out there ready to follow you, Peter. Aslan obviously believed you could. And so do I,"

The fire in Edmund's heart, put there by Aslan, appeared in Peter's eyes. His words had worked. Peter would lead them in battle against evil!

As Peter instructed the captains of the army, Edmund stood by him ready to offer support and advice. He didn't mind being the little brother of the leader; he was happy and proud to be able to help Peter in any way that he could. He felt that he was the old Edmund he used to be, before he became so concerned about showing people how grown up he was. It felt very good. Even though the battle would be very dangerous, deep down Edmund thought that, even if he died, he was still pleased that he came to Narnia because he had managed to find his true self again.

As the captains moved to prepare their forces for the battle, Oreius spoke to him.

"Your brother wants you to oversee the archers and hold the high ground. He has great faith in you."

Edmund glowed inside. He had won his brother's love and respect. He had been forgiven. There was only one person's forgiveness Edmund now needed. His own.

Taking his place with the archers, Edmund saw the White Witch's army of dreadful monsters and evil beasts approach. Her army was larger than Peter's, yet Edmund still had the faith and hope put in his heart by Aslan. This belief meant that, though he was frightened, he did not despair.

It was time to fight

Edmund watched a gryphon swoop over the battlefield and land by Peter.

"They come, your Highness. In numbers and weapons far greater than our own," said the gryphon.

"Numbers do not win a battle," counselled Oreius.

Peter looked at the Witch's army. "No, but I bet they help," he said.

Facing the Witch, Peter raised his sword in challenge and the army cheered.

Peter pointed his sword toward the enemy and cried "For Narnia... and for Aslan!"

No one cheered louder than Edmund and then... the battle began.

Peter's first move against the Witch's army was to have the eagles, hawks and other birds drop rocks from the sky. After the birds had attacked, Peter took his army into the battle. Edmund watched them go and ordered his archers to shoot.

The battle raged and as the sides fought, Edmund kept a close eye on his brother. He also watched with horror as the White Witch turned fauns, centaurs and other good creatures into stone statues. It was difficult to tell who was winning; Edmund tried his best to make sure that the archers prevented the Witch's army from making it up the hill. He remembered from history lessons that it was important for the defending army to keep the high ground.

Then Edmund saw something that shook his body to the core. Peter was stranded and surrounded by monsters and the White Witch herself was stalking straight for Peter. Edmund wasn't going to allow his brother to be turned to stone! Not while there was breath in his body!

Edmund had to fight his way past many of the White Witch's monsters but he never took his eyes off Peter and the Witch. He had to reach her before she got close enough to use her wand on Peter. He had to. There was no way he could fail.

The Witch moved closer and closer to Peter. Still Peter didn't turn around. The Witch moved closer. Edmund pushed harder, forcing monsters out of the way. The Witch raised her wand …

Edmund was too far to do anything unless … there was only one thing he could do …

With a mighty effort, Edmund leapt. The world began to move in slow motion. He could see his feet leaving the ground. He could see the Witch and her wand moving; the end was sparkling with her evil magic. Edmund saw his own sword in his hand. This was his only chance and he must not fail this time.

Edmund's sword came crashing down and broke the White Witch's wand in two. He had saved Peter! The Witch screamed a terrifying scream that could make the very blood run cold in your veins. With great anger and venom in her eyes, she stabbed Edmund with the broken wand.

And Edmund felt … cold. Very cold.

The battle continued but to Edmund it sounded as though it was very far away. He heard his brother Peter shout, "no!" But the shout sounded like a shout from another world. Everything was getting darker and colder. Edmund wasn't sure where he was. It felt as though he was lying in snow. He couldn't make any sense of what he could see. The battle was a blur. It was moving too fast for him to understand. And he was tired. So tired, that he could not keep his eyes open any longer.

He was not sad though. He was pleased. He was pleased that he had saved his brother, and learnt how to be brave.

As Edmund's eyes began to close he thought to himself, I must be dreaming. It looks as though Aslan has returned. Through his half closed eyes he saw the King of Narnia pounce on the White Witch. Then his eyes closed and all he saw was darkness.

There was something warm in Edmund's mouth. It tasted like honey but was hot. In fact, it was heating his whole body. Suddenly, his eyes were open again and there in front of him was Lucy. She had saved him with her magical cordial.

Edmund looked around. His family were all safe and sound. Aslan had returned! It hadn't been a dream. The White Witch had been defeated by the mighty Lion. Edmund watched with joy as Aslan marched around the battlefield using his breath to bring all the statues back to life. He was sorry to have missed the final moments of the battle, but was grateful that he and his brother and sisters and all the good creatures of Narnia were alive and free. Yes, it was victory.

Years later, all four of the Kings and Queens of Narnia were riding to find the magical white stag. They rode for a long time. Edmund began to think that if they rode much further they would surely leave Narnia and fall off the edge of the world.

Instead, they came across a metal tree with a light at the top. It seemed familiar to Edmund, but he couldn't remember why. It was like an old photo from long ago. The Kings and Queens got off their horses and pushed through the thick forest. Edmund was beginning to remember a story he had heard, about four children who found a world inside a wardrobe. He was about to ask his brother and sisters if they remembered the story as well when he suddenly noticed that the tree in front of him was not a tree but a coat… then the ground vanished underneath his feet and all four of the Kings and Queens were tumbling towards a strange light.

Seconds later, Edmund, a child once more, fell out of the wardrobe with his older brother and two sisters. All four of them collapsed in a pile together. Then Edmund remembered, this was their world. It seemed strange to him to be back and to suddenly be young again, after living in Narnia for so many years as a King. But it still felt good. Edmund smiled and looked at his brother and sisters. He knew now that being with them was the only thing that really mattered at all.